# *Picture*
# HIM

## Jo Cotterill

Rans⬤m

# ONE

I look very hard at the computer.
One of my photos fills the
screen. It is of a plastic bag
stuck in a tree, blown by the wind
and now trapped. The white
plastic billows like a sail.

My friend Zoe is sitting next to me.
She brushes her blonde hair out of
her eyes and makes a sort of huffing
noise.

'You are SO weird, Aliya. Who
takes photos of plastic bags?'

'I do,' I say. 'I like p-plastic
b-b-bags. B-b-b-b … '

Zoe waits. I have a stammer, and
sometimes it takes me a very long
time to say what I want. Lots of
people don't stick around to listen.
But Zoe does.

'B-b-b-because,' I say, with relief, 'they can b-b-be so many things. Like b-b-b-b … '

I give up. I want to say 'boats' and then 'balloons', but to be honest, we haven't got all day for me to get the words out.

I shrug instead. Zoe grins in understanding.

I love taking photos because it's easier than talking. And sometimes it's a great excuse to get away from a conversation.

If someone asks me a question and I can't get the words out, I just lift my camera instead and start taking photos.

Or I pretend I've spotted
something amazing in the distance
and run off to take a picture.

'When are you going to shoot me again?'

Zoe looks hopeful. It's great that she's my best friend. I love taking photos and she loves being in them!

'Well,' I say, 'there's the exhibition in three weeks. You know, the one the art dep-p-p-partment has every year. I was thinking I might do zombie p-p-princess.'

Zoe's eyes open wide.

'OMG YES! Can I be your model? With a tiara and ballgown and blood running down my arms?'

I laugh. Zoe is up for anything that means dressing up. 'You so can.'

A boy comes into the photography studio. He has dark hair that falls into his eyes, and he leans forward, like he's trying to hide from the world.

He sees me and Zoe, looks away, and then leaves.

Zoe rolls her eyes. 'Ben is SO weird.'

'He never speaks to me,' I say, shaking my head. 'We've b-b-been in the same class for two years and I d-d-don't think he's even said hello.'

'Sad,' says Zoe.

'B-b-but his pictures are amazing,' I say.

I look up. On the wall above this computer is one of Ben's photos. It's of a bridge over a river in the rain.

The water is all dimpled, and you can even see the rain bouncing off a leaf. It's a really clever photo.

'Whatever,' says Zoe. 'You camera people are all odd. Now, when do I get to dress up as a zombie princess?'

# TWO

It's three days later and Zoe and I are walking to the site for the zombie princess photo shoot.

'This skirt is so heavy,' Zoe complains, panting.

She is wearing a long vintage dress
that I bought from a charity shop.
We added some fake pearls to
make it look more princessy.

And Zoe borrowed her mum's
wedding tiara, promising not to
damage it on pain of death. Or pain
of no allowance, anyway.

I have chosen a place on the edge of the local park. It's got a tangle of trees next to a sort of pond.

It's the bit of the park that gets forgotten about – the bit where kids go to drink and smoke and snog.

It's a cloudy day, which suits me fine because when you're taking photos outside, you don't want bright sunshine. It makes the photos too white, and any people in the picture will screw up their eyes.

Zoe starts to apply her fake blood. I set up my tripod, which I borrowed from school. Then I fix my camera to the top of it. I have already been here to work out what kinds of shots I want to take.

When Zoe is ready, I start shooting. She looks amazing, like a crazy bride. And then I spot an empty beer can lying on the ground, so I use it as the focus of my next shot, blurring the image of Zoe in the background.

I get totally into the zone, moving

my camera around to get shots from all sides. Zoe is great at acting, so she does blank zombie, frightened zombie and full-on flesh-eating zombie. She's awesome! My pictures are going to be amazing!

But very, very slowly, I start to feel odd. Like someone or something is watching me. You know that prickle at the back of your neck? I get that.

I look around. There are two people lying on a blanket in the park. They're listening to music and laughing. It's not them.

A man is walking his dog along the path. It's not him.

Why do I feel like I'm being watched?

'What's the matter?' asks Zoe.

I shake myself. 'Do you ... do you feel like someone's watching you?'

Zoe grins. 'Only you and your camera!'

I must be imagining things.

# THREE

It's not until the next morning that
I get a chance to edit my photos at
school.

I have over 500 to check!

I am so pleased with them; it's going to be really hard to choose the best.

Mr Berry, my teacher, comes over to see. 'These are brilliant, Aliya,' he says. 'I love the way you've composed the shots. They have a lot of atmosphere.'

I am proud he likes them. Atmosphere is important in good photos.

A good photo should make you *feel* something when you look at it.

'This one,' says Mr Berry, pointing at the screen, 'with the empty can, is really great. And the figure in shadow behind your zombie princess adds to the menace.'

I feel very cold.

The figure *behind* Zoe? But –
there was no one there ...

Mr Berry nods and moves over to
talk to Ben on the other side of the
room.

Fingers shaking, I zoom in on the
part of the photo Mr Berry pointed
to.

There *is* a figure. It's blurred.
I can't tell if it's a boy or a girl, or how
old or anything. I can't even see
what it's wearing because it's only in
shadow.

But there is definitely a face, and a body, and legs ... and it's just standing there, watching us.

I can't move.

Who is it? *That's* why I felt there was someone watching me!

In a panic, I scroll through the rest of the images from the shoot.

He – or she – isn't there all the time, but in the background of some of the shots ... yes. The figure in shadow.

And then, without even thinking about it, I start looking through my other photo albums. The collection of photos of the plastic bag. Some close-ups of flowers. Reflections of trees in puddles.

Every so often, there is a figure in shadow in the background.

I am being watched.

# FOUR

'Oh my GOD,' says Zoe when I tell her at lunch. 'You have a stalker? That's, like, freaky! Can you see who it is?'

'N-n-no,' I say, and I hold out

some photos
I have printed
out.

My hands are
still shaking and I
feel sick. 'Look.'

Zoe looks at the photos. 'These are all in different places. Jeez, he's been following you for ages!'

I nod, miserable.

'You can't zoom in any closer?' Zoe asks.

I shake my head. 'He's n-not in focus. There's n-no way to make it cl … clearer. How can I not have s-s-seen him when I was taking the photos?'

'Aliya, you don't see *anything*

when you're shooting,' Zoe tells me. 'You only see what's in the lens. A double-decker bus could be coming at you and you wouldn't notice it.'

She gives me a big hug. 'You should tell the police. Show them the pictures.'

'The p-p-p-p ... !' I can't even get the word out.

I shake my head. 'No way.' I can't tell the police. I can hardly speak to my friend! The idea of trying to explain to police, with my stammer ... I would rather stick my head in a fire.

I stare out at the playground. It's full of kids. Am I being watched right now?

I shiver. How will I dare leave my house?

'What a tosser,' Zoe says, looking at the photos again. 'He must be sick.'

At her words, something inside me feels angry.

How dare this PERSON follow me around?

How dare he sneak into my photos??

How dare he frighten me like this???...

I sit up straight. I take a slow breath.

'I'm not going to the p ... police,' I say. 'I want to catch him. Get him on camera.'

I turn to my friend. 'Will you help me?' I ask, and I don't stumble over any of the sounds.

Zoe presses her lips together and nods. She looks fierce.

'Just tell me what to do.'

# FIVE

That afternoon, Zoe and I talk in loud voices about doing another photo shoot.

People in class tell us to shut up, but we don't care. What if the stalker gets his information from someone at school? We need him to know where we'll be.

I tell my mum I'm doing an evening shoot with Zoe. She nods and tells me not to be late home. My tummy is flipping like a pancake, I am so nervous.

Zoe and I meet at the children's playground, which is empty. I ask her to sit down on one of the swings.

I look around, afraid. The main road isn't far away, and Zoe and I have a plan for if it all goes wrong. Run very fast, basically.

I start taking photos. I don't have the tripod this time. It would be too hard to carry if I have to run.

Very soon, I know he's here. I can feel it. I keep snapping, but I change the settings on my camera.

Now everything in the background is in sharp focus.

Zoe is blurred in the lens as she looks at me, but I can see the grass and the trees beyond. They are crystal clear.

And so is the figure as he leans
out from behind a tree.

I gasp and nearly drop my
camera. Then I look at the photo I've
just taken. I can zoom in on the
screen ... right in on the face of the
figure ...

And then I gasp again.

It's Ben.

# SIX

I am so angry I don't hesitate. I leave Zoe on the swings and march across the playground, past the climbing frame, past the roundabout.

The figure ducks behind the tree.

'I know it's you!' I shout as I head towards him. 'Come out, you coward! I saw you through my camera, Ben, I know it's you!'

Behind me, I hear Zoe repeat, '*Ben?*' and then come running after me.

He steps out, his dark hair hanging across his eyes. He's wearing the same grey hoodie as in all my photos. He looks at the ground.

'What the hell are you doing?' I shout at him. 'How dare you follow me everywhere? Who do you think you are?' In my anger, my stammer has completely disappeared.

Ben backs away. 'I'm sorry,' he mutters. 'I didn't mean ... I just ... '

'You just WHAT?' I scream. 'Want to freak me out? Want to make me scared of my own shadow?'

Zoe catches us up and stands beside me.

'I just ...' he says quietly, 'I just like you.'

I am stunned. 'You are *nuts*. You *like* me? That is *not* the way to show it, Ben. For goodness' sake! I thought you were a creepy stalker! You think this makes me *like* you?'

I shake my head. 'Don't come near me again. Seriously. Or I'm going to the police.'

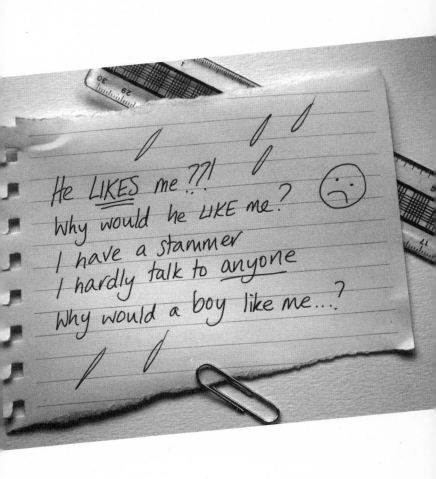

# SEVEN

It's a week later. I haven't seen Ben
since I shouted at him, which is a
relief. I am in the big art room putting
together my zombie princess display
for the exhibition.

Mr Berry comes by and stops to look. 'That's wonderful,' he tells me. 'You've got such a good eye, Aliya. It's a rare thing to have. You and Ben are the only two students in your year to have such talent.'

He sighs. 'Such a shame, what happened to that family.'

I frown. 'What d-d-do you mean, *what happened*?'

'I thought everyone knew,' Mr Berry says. 'Ben's sister was killed in a car accident a year ago. He used to be such a happy, cheerful lad. But now he hardly talks to anyone. It's like he's forgotten what it's like to be happy or have friends.'

He sighs again. 'A week ago, I asked him if he'd like to make a tribute to his sister for the exhibition, but it was the wrong thing to say. He's been missing lessons. I worry that we're losing him.'

He nods at my pictures. 'You keep on doing what you do. You're turning into a really good photographer.'

He goes out, but any pride I have in my work has gone. I feel very, very sad – and kind of guilty. I mean, Ben shouldn't have followed me around. It was weird and creepy. But maybe it was because he didn't know how to talk to me.

When the exhibition opens, everyone is very kind about my zombie princess photos.

But the display no one can stop talking about is Ben's. It covers the whole of the end wall – hundreds and hundreds of photos.

They are all pictures of rain – raindrops on windows, in mid-air, hanging from leaves …

It's like a wall of tears.

But that's not the most amazing thing. Right in the middle, so that you don't see it unless you're looking right at it, is a photo of a plastic bag in a tree.

And I know it's his way of saying sorry.

# EIGHT

'You're insane,' Zoe tells me the next day. 'I don't understand.'

I smile. 'I know. B-b-but he needs me. He's asking for m-m-my help.'

No one has ever asked *me* for help before.

It feels ... different.

I post the note into Ben's school locker.

It says:

I don't like
talking
much.
But if you want to
sit
with me
some time
and not talk
that would be
nice.
We could look
at
plastic bags in trees
And
maybe
walk in the rain.

I haven't written my name.

He'll know who it's from.

## ch@t

by Barbara Catchpole

'Are you out of your tiny looney-tunes mind?'

That's what Gina's sister says when she finds out Gina is chatting online with a boy she doesn't know.

But Gina loves talking to Chatboy1 – he makes her laugh and he *understands* her. But what will happen when Gina tries to meet him IRL?

## I ♥ Glitter Boy

by Julia Clark

Lily loves bling – and she loves Mark Ward. He just doesn't know it – yet ...

But he will, as soon as he opens her love letter to him, filled with shiny, pink glitter.

The only problem is, the glitter spills all over him and won't come off.

How can Lily win Glitter Boy's heart now?